A Boy's

A Boy's Boat

By Bruce Holaday
Illustrated by Ian Grabinski

From the Prairie Publications, Inc.
South Bend, Indiana

From the Prairie Publications, Inc., books are available at quantity discounts with bulk purchase of educational, business, or sales pro-motional use. For information about discounts, please go to http://ftppublications.wixsite.com/ftpp.

Book cover design by Miguel Quijada
of MQ Graphic Design Solutions

Library of Congress Control Number: 2017935248

Printed in the United States of America
ISBN-13: 978-0-9972817-9-8
ISBN-10: 0-9972817-9-0

For Claire

Illustrations

Prologue

Each June, the half-moon-shaped cove reawakened to life as it had year after year for centuries. The big lake's little nursery of fish, turtles, snakes, frogs, bugs, birds, ducks, snails, and minnows hatched from pink, white, gray, blue, and yellow eggs of varying sizes and shapes and began their childhood in the shallow, sun-warmed waters. Muskrats and weasels snuggled around their babies in fur-lined dens under the shoreline maze of tree roots and happily awoke to the new day from dreams of fresh eggs and plentiful fish. Young and eager life flourished in the cove once again after a dark, still winter of ice and snow.

As the morning breeze picked up over the deep, green water of the lake, waves rolled toward the cove, flattening out and becoming only ripples as they washed into the shallow water. Barely two feet deep throughout most of the cove, the clear water bent the early morning sunlight into ribbons of sparkling white and yellow, reflecting off the soft sand below.

From out of the thick woods, hundreds of birds gathered along the shore, awakening the cove with cheerful singing, but also with scolding in defense of their nests, eggs, and hatchlings. Shy Great Blue Herons waded silently near the shore on long skinny legs, their sharp beaks poised to grab minnow breakfasts. The loud snare drum report of a kingfisher echoed off the dense wall of the woods as she flew from one overhanging limb to another. Skipjack minnows that had hatched weeks earlier, schooled in undulating clouds of thousands as all the watery predators chased them.

As the sun burned off the morning chill, fishermen's motorboats could be heard roaring just outside the cove, relegated to water deep enough to safeguard their saw-blade-like propellers. Few boats ever purposefully crossed over the outer ledge of the cove, save for an occasional fisherman in a canoe or kayak who had to paddle far to get there. The shallow water of the cove protected the nursery on one side, and the dense shoreline woods protected it on the other.

Over the years, Jack's grandfather had purchased all the land from one end of the cove to the other to guarantee that the woods and shoreline would always be home to the birds, fish, and animals. Grandfather's little three-room log cabin sat in a half-acre, grassy clearing almost exactly in the middle of the cove. A weathered, twenty-two-foot-long, gray-wood dock protruded from the land, over the shoreline, out into the water. There was no point to having a longer dock. It could have been a thousand feet long and still the water in the shade of the dock boards would have been only two feet deep and in some spots even shallower.

Early summer had awakened. New life had awakened. The morning had awakened. Jack was just awakening too.

Chapter One

Somewhere between dreams and awakening to full consciousness, Jack smelled bacon cooking and toast too. The day's first thought sparked: *I hope there is orange juice.*

In less than a second, that thought was lost to the human reflex reminding him where he was, why he was there, who was also there, and that he was safe. Jack sat up in bed and remembered that Grandfather was an early riser too. Probably Grandfather was cooking the bacon, so Jack went to see.

The cabin's only large room faced the lake and included the kitchen, an eating area, and the living room with a stone fireplace. Behind it, toward the back, were his grandparents' bedroom and the bathroom. Jack slept above their bedroom in an open loft from which he could look down into the kitchen and living room.

He smiled as he saw his grandfather flipping the bacon in the skillet, and said, "Smells good."

His grandfather looked up to the loft, smiled at Jack, and said, "Be ready in just a few, Skipper. C'mon down."

Jack had visited his grandparents at the cabin on weekends for many summers, but always with his parents and older sister. This summer was different. Change was awakening, and though Jack felt it, he did not really think about it in words.

His mother had been offered a new job in a town about forty miles from where they lived. His parents had decided that it was a good opportunity, so they were selling the house and moving. It was going to be a busy summer for his parents, so they had decided that it would be better for all if Jack and his sister spent a few weeks away during the move.

Jack's sister loved the idea of attending a sleepover, riding camp. She imagined herself riding horses every day, so she had eagerly agreed. Jack's parents talked to him about several different camps, but Jack somehow sensed that they really wanted him to spend the weeks with Grandfather and Grandmother at the cabin. Jack had always liked being at the lake and remembered swimming in the cove, pulling up radishes from Grandfather's garden, and trying to figure out which carrots were the biggest before tugging them from the ground.

He had told his parents, "Yeah, I can go to the lake, but if you need help, I'll come back to give you a hand." He thought that the little smiles his parents exchanged were a bit odd, but he did not think about it for long. Actually, they knew something special awaited Jack at the cove that summer.

"You hungry, Skipper?" Grandfather asked.

"I guess," Jack replied. "Do you have orange juice?"

"You bet," Grandfather said. "Coming right up."

Jack's grandmother came out of the bedroom, soon after, in her red robe and soft blue slippers. "It's wonderful to see you this bright, sunny morning, Jack," she said, smiling broadly, while kissing him on the forehead. "You've grown so much since we last saw you."

Jack knew that was a good thing. He blushed just a little and took a bite of the warm toast with a bit too much jelly on it.

"I've lost track, Jack. How old are you now?" Grandfather asked.

"Eleven, but almost twelve," Jack said.

"Hmm, thought so," Grandfather replied, with no visible expression.

Grandmother couldn't help herself and laughed a bit too loudly for the moment. She turned her eyes down to the floor and walked quickly over to the sink.

Jack was a perceptive boy. "What's up?" he asked. "What's the secret?"

"Not a secret, really, Jack," Grandfather said pleasantly. "It's just that I have something to show you."

"Let him finish his breakfast at least, Allan," said Jack's grandmother.

"I'm full—really," Jack said, his curiosity piqued. "What is it?"

"Well, okay," Grandfather said. "Let's head out to the shed. You ready?" They left the table full of plates and glasses because today was special and dirty dishes simply didn't matter.

Chapter Two

The shed had been used in years past as a car garage, but it had long since been the place where everything Grandfather didn't know where to store ended up. Always the last to get a fresh coat of paint or any real maintenance, the shed was rough and cluttered with all sorts of tools, discarded paint buckets, scraps of wood, a workbench with a wood vise, old lawn mowers, and cobwebs. Jack remembered it well. He liked it. It was a place where he could find wood to hammer nails into. Just last summer, he had found a board in the shed that he sawed to length and used a rasp to carve it into a boat-like shape he had played with in the shallow water.

As they approached the shed, John came up from the lake, where he had been working on the annual repairs of the old dock. Nearly as old as Grandfather but a larger man, John lived near the lake year round and helped Jack's grandfather take care of the cabin and dock. He watched over the place during the off-season and helped fix everything that needed attention. Jack wasn't exactly sure what to make of John, primarily because John was always so quiet and kept mostly to himself, but he knew that John and Grandfather were friends, and that was good enough.

"Perfect timing, John," Grandfather called out.

"Wouldn't miss this," replied John with a broad smile that Jack thought was very much out of character.

They reached the shed, and as Grandfather and John started to pull back the folding garage doors on their rusty hinges, Grandfather paused and said to Jack, "So, I think you're old enough now to be the skipper of your own boat. This winter, I built this for you."

As the doors creaked open, there in the shadows of the shed was the prettiest little dinghy Jack had ever seen. Even in the dark of the windowless shed, the sunny-yellow sheer plank and glossy-white topsides made all three smile. The varnished seats, the copper bow plate, and brass, keel-rub strake shone in the dim light. Jack slowly walked into the shed and ran his hand along the varnished gunwales.

Jack was speechless. A flood of joy filled his small body. He couldn't say anything right away. Then, finally he said, "You made this for me?"

"Yes, Jack," Grandfather replied.

5

It had taken nine months of shaping, sanding, fitting, worrying, cursing, skinning knuckles, more sanding, painting, sanding, and even more sanding. Now, at this moment, Grandfather knew that all the work had been worth the effort. He was, simply, happy. He had built a boat. He had built a boat for his grandson.

Jack was so excited that he could not help bouncing up and down a bit as John and Grandfather lifted the tongue of the trailer and walked the dinghy out of the shed into the sunlight. Grandfather had agonized over every detail from the oar leathers to the whipping of each line. He had polished the brass and even waxed the brightwork so that the vessel would look her best for launching. His pride showed in his sparkling eyes, and Jack felt it and was happy.

They had rolled her down to the shoreline, right to the edge of the water, when, still in her robe and slippers, Grandmother came running out of the cabin.

"Allan!" she called to Grandfather.

"Oh, sorry, Kate," Grandfather called back to Grandmother. "Just got ahead of ourselves a bit."

"Well, we're going to do this right, you know," Grandmother said with determination.

"Yes, absolutely," Grandfather replied with a smile.

With that, Grandmother said, "Jack, the name of your boat is *Petit Bateau*. Do you know what that means?"

Jack shook his head.

"It means little boat, in French," she said.

"Your grandmother was a French professor at the university," Grandfather interjected, proudly. "She picked the name."

"Jack," Grandmother went on, "a little boat is the best boat. Do you know why?"

Jack didn't know what exactly to say.

"When the young men go to Annapolis to join the Navy, the first thing they have to learn is how to sail a small boat," she started to explain. "A small boat teaches you about wind and waves. A big boat is just a log in the water. *Petit Bateau* will be a lively and fun way to learn how to be a true seaman. That's why a small boat is the best."

With that said, Grandmother showed what was behind her back, a bottle that Jack knew was wine of some sort. She opened the champagne bottle with a pop and then paused. She said slowly and quietly, "God bless this little boat, *Petit Bateau*, and all who sail in her." With that, she poured a little champagne on the copper bow plate of *Petit Bateau* and then laughed. Grandfather and John smiled and took ahold of the dinghy on both sides.

"Jack, grab the bow," said Grandfather.

They lifted her off the trailer, walked a few feet down to the water's edge, and gently floated her out onto the lake. *Petit Bateau* was launched, and Jack felt in his heart how special this moment was. He had just been given his own boat. *Petit Bateau* was his.

Chapter Three

"You hold her there, and I'll go get the oars," said Grandfather over his shoulder as he walked back up to the shed. As he passed Grandmother, she reached out and touched his hand.

"Well, I have a kitchen to clean up," Grandmother said with a smile. "Anchors aweigh, Jack!

"I should be getting back to work on the dock," said John as he let go of the starboard side of *Petit Bateau* and left Jack with his new boat. As he stood in the knee-deep water with his hands holding onto the port gunwale, Jack just had to push down and pull up on the side a few times, as if to awaken the sleeping boat to life. She rocked gently in the calm water, and small ripples undulated from both sides of the hull. Jack laughed aloud.

At this moment, when Jack and *Petit Bateau* were alone for the first time, Jack began to know his boat. He felt the smoothness of the varnished, center seat and realized that the thin, vertical box with a narrow slot in the top, right in front of the seat, was a dagger board trunk. "She's a sailboat too!" Jack yelled with excitement to John, who had begun to pound nails into a dock board.

John looked up and simply gave Jack a "thumbs up" and a smile.

Jack let go of *Petit Bateau* and stepped back a couple of feet to take her all in. She floated so lightly, as if she displaced less than an inch of water. Her shadow on the sand two feet below mirrored the shape of her hull.

Petit Bateau's 11-foot-2-inch length seemed much longer to Jack as he held onto her lightly and waded around to her stern. There, in shiny gold letters, *Petit Bateau* arced to match the curve of the top of the transom. Jack saw that the gray paint on the floor looked rough, and he knew that it was nonskid paint so he wouldn't slip when it was wet, as dinghies often are. Jack wanted to get into his boat right then, and he looked up to see Grandfather coming out of the shed.

Grandfather came back, hauling two varnished oars with tan oar leathers and stops. The bronze oar rings had slipped down past the leathers, and Jack noticed that they were free to move up and down the oars until they hit the stops, but he wasn't sure what that meant. Grandfather also had a red life jacket under one arm, and Jack thought that he certainly wasn't going to wear that.

"Can we sail her today?" Jack asked with excitement in his voice.

"Well, yes, I guess," Grandfather answered a bit slowly, "but I really was hoping to get another coat or two of varnish on the spars. Do you mind waiting a couple of days for the first sail?"

"No, that's all right," Jack replied. "Can I get in now?"

"Absolutely!" Grandfather answered with gusto.

With both hands on the port gunwale, Jack pushed down to lift himself up over the rail, and *Petit Bateau* responded as she was designed by heeling over considerably to the point that Jack lost his balance, let go, and stumbled back into the water almost falling backwards, but catching himself before an embarrassing fall that would have left him soaked and seated on the sandy bottom.

Grandfather laughed aloud, and for a second, Jack thought he was laughing at him and felt odd, but then Grandfather yelled over to John, "She is tender and lively just as you predicted, John. Isn't that great?" Grandfather wasn't laughing at Jack. He was just happy that *Petit Bateau* heeled and balanced lightly. Jack wasn't so sure that a boat that heeled so easily was a good thing.

"In a small boat, you need to get your weight toward the center as you climb in," Grandfather explained.

"Okay, so hold the other side while I get in," Jack requested.

Grandfather paused for a moment and then said, "Yes, that would help, but maybe it would be better to do it on your own. When you're off having adventures all over the cove, I won't be there to help."

Jack had not thought that far ahead. He suddenly imagined himself rowing to the far ends of the cove, sailing out into the lake, and being an explorer of places he had not seen before. He positioned his hands on the seat as close to the center of the boat as he could and swung his right leg up over the gunwale. His first boarding of *Petit Bateau* was a mix of sliding, tumbling, and rolling, but he laughed and scrambled up onto the seat.

"Good job, Skipper," Grandfather said. "Ready to go rowing?"

"This is so cool!" Jack said.

Grandfather slipped the brass oar rings back up onto the leathers and inserted them into the oarlocks on each side. Jack took an oar in each hand, while the blades bobbed lightly in the water. Jack was about to pull on an oar for the first time when Grandfather said, "Oh, and let's put on the life jacket first."

Jack looked at Grandfather with a little incredulity and said, "So, I'm in the water without a life jacket, but then when I'm in a boat, I have to wear one?"

Grandfather laughed and said, "You're a clever fellow, but let's do this..." and he hesitated before finishing his sentence, "for me." Jack looked up toward the cabin and saw Grandmother watching.

"Fine," Jack said.

As Grandfather waded toward the shore, Jack pulled on one oar and then the other. *Petit Bateau* responded instantly and swerved a little from side to side. One oar angled too deeply and dug down into the water, almost touching the sand. The other angled too shallowly and pulled up out of the water. Jack focused on the blade ends of the oars and watched them intently as he pulled. He adjusted his grip, and just as every young boy has done since there were dinghies and young boys, Jack began to learn how to row.

"Let's stay pretty close to the dock today—please," Grandfather called out to him.

"Okay," said Jack.

When Grandfather walked out onto the dock where John had just nailed down a new board, he stood for a moment watching Jack row and said, "Do you see how light and swift she is?"

John stood up, smiled, and said, "She floats like a feather. She's going to be a great boat for Jack. Good job, Al."

Grandfather felt pride well up inside, and he blushed a bit and said, "Thanks."

The morning had turned out exactly as Grandfather had imagined many times while he built her all those months. Jack and *Petit Bateau* were perfect for each other.

Chapter Four

"Well, last weekend's rain gave the weeds in the garden a fresh lease on life. I had better get to work, or I won't be able to find the carrots before long," Grandfather said to John and laughed. He watched Jack row *Petit Bateau* for a minute more. Then he added, "You got him?"

John nodded once and replied, "Of course."

A curious thing happens when a boy rows his boat. Time disappears. Jack couldn't tell if he had been rowing for half an hour or an hour. Actually, he and *Petit Bateau* had been playing in the morning light for nearly two hours, getting to know each other and becoming friends.

At first, Jack tried to row as fast as he could, occasionally digging an oar in too deeply, with the boat's momentum pushing the oar back hard into him. Sometimes, he lost concentration, and an oar would only skim over the top of the water and produce little forward thrust. Then at other times, Jack simply watched the wake fan out from behind his boat into an expanding "V" shape, and he settled into a rhythm that suited *Petit Bateau*, gliding along smoothly and in silence.

Rowing can be hard work, and Jack had pulled hard enough to lift himself up off the seat for several strokes when his arms began to feel tired, and he needed to rest a bit. He pushed down on the oar handles and, as the blades lifted out of the water, *Petit Bateau* still coasted along. He watched the crystal water droplets fall from the tip of each oar and make a string of little bull's-eyes trailing away from the slowing boat. When he pushed the handles even lower, the drops of water ran all the way down the oars, onto Jack's hands, and into the bottom of the boat.

There are many things to do in a small boat besides just rowing along. Jack pulled on one oar and pushed on the other, and the little boat swung around within her own length. He turned the starboard oar flat on top of the water and smacked the surface of the water hard. He was pleased with how loud it sounded echoing off into the woods, but a Great Blue Heron along the shore thought otherwise and flew a few hundred yards farther away. Jack learned how to scrape the top inch off the water with a fast pull on the oar and send a tall spray of water aft. He couldn't help but think about whom he might want to surprise with a splash or two. He quickly decided it would be his sister. She would be with them when his parents came to pick him up.

He stood up in *Petit Bateau* and felt how easy it was to rock her back and forth. He planted his feet solidly toward each side and shoved down with one leg and then the other. The little boat responded instantly, rolling and sending out ripples. He steadied her out and sat down on the aft seat, arms spread wide to each gunwale and his back against the transom. The bow rose up out of the water a few inches. He smiled and thought to himself: *My own boat. Awesome!*

He went back toward the bow, stopping to peer down into the dagger board trunk slot. The thin streak of water at the bottom looked surprisingly bright and a lighter shade of green than the water surrounding the boat. Jack liked how bright the sliver of water looked inside the trunk.

As he walked farther forward, *Petit Bateau* became less stable, and Jack instinctively lowered his body and held onto the gunwales. He sat facing forward on the bow seat and turned to see the stern rising several inches higher than before. He pivoted around and walked back to the center seat and took ahold of the oars.

Just as he turned *Petit Bateau* back toward the dock and looked over his shoulder to see if he was lined up to start rowing, he saw Grandmother about halfway between the cabin and the shore. She was talking to John and waving. John waved back to her, turned, and waved at Jack to come in.

"Already?" Jack said to himself.

With a few smooth, steady, but strong strokes, *Petit Bateau* came up to speed and glided toward home. In fewer than five minutes, Jack was holding the oars steadily in the water to slow her down and aiming her right at John on the dock. He hadn't started "holding water" early enough, though, and came into the dock faster than he had intended. John reached out with his strong arms and caught *Petit Bateau* just before she hit the dock.

"Might want to come in a little easier next time," John remarked casually.

"Yeah," Jack replied. "Sorry."

John swung the boat alongside the dock so Jack could jump out.

"We can just tie her by the bow for now," said John. "She will hang downwind away from the dock and be okay."

Jack watched as John slipped the bowline between the dock boards and backed up again. He seemed to flip the line around and twist it, and the result was a knot that held *Petit Bateau* securely.

"How did you do that?" asked Jack.

"Well, the knot is spelled just like bowline," explained John. "But it is pronounced 'bo-lin.' It's the best knot to use for the bowline because you can always get it undone no matter how hard the boat has pulled on it."

"Yes, John, the rabbit comes up out of the hole, around the tree, and back down again," said Grandmother with a laugh. She had come all the way out onto the dock. "Really, you must save that lengthy lesson for a bit later, John. I've made a special lunch for everyone, so let's get up to the house."

John waited behind to make sure that *Petit Bateau* was hanging off the dock safely. As Grandmother walked toward the cabin with Jack, she asked, "Well, do you like her?"

Jack grinned and said, "It's such a cool boat. I can't believe it. This is going to be the best summer ever. I can't wait to sail her. Did you see how fast I was going? I rocked her back and forth. I'm going to spray Anna when she gets here. It's so cool."

Grandmother laughed and said, "That's wonderful, honey." She paused for a moment, stopped walking, and quietly added, "Did you thank your grandfather for giving you this gift?"

Jack's heart sank instantly. His face went gray, and he felt a little sick to his stomach. "I, I, I did, yes. I think I did. I meant to," he stammered.

"Well, it might be nice to say it again," Grandmother suggested. Besides, it would be helpful if you went out to the garden and told Grandfather that lunch is on the table."

"Okay," Jack said. He started to run and then slowed down as he collected his thoughts. When he got to the garden, Grandfather was on his knees pulling weeds from around the carrots and radishes. Jack walked up slowly and said, "Hi."

"Hey, Skipper. How did it go?" Grandfather asked, turning away from his garden to face Jack.

"Grandfather?" Jack replied.

"Yes?" Grandfather responded.

Jack had planned the words while walking to the garden, but no words came out at that moment. Tears welled up, and Jack simply lunged forward and hugged his grandfather. He wanted to thank his grandfather, but he also felt shame and embarrassment for not thanking him sooner.

Chapter Five

Words can be very useful, but Jack's hug meant more to Grandfather at that moment. He returned Jack's hug strongly, and the back of his throat tightened up while the back of his eyes itched a bit. He coughed it off, as most grown men do at such times and said slowly and kindly, "You are most welcome, Skipper." He had to cough one more time and then said, "I suspect your grandmother has lunch ready. Shall we see what's the big surprise?"

Jack nodded, and together, they walked to the cabin, Grandfather's arm a bit too tight around Jack's shoulder.

"Uh, I think my arms are already sore from rowing," said Jack.

Grandfather laughed, loosened his grip on Jack, and said, "In a couple of weeks, you will be the strongest rower in the cove."

Jack laughed at that and replied, "I'll still be the only rower in the cove."

They walked to the cabin together.

"Ta da!" Grandmother announced as she set the plate of sandwiches on the table in front of Grandfather, John, and Jack. The three smiled, almost too widely, and looked at each other. "Well?" Grandmother asked.

"Well, thanks, Kate," Grandfather began slowly. "The peanut butter and jelly sandwiches look, uh, good."

"You don't get it," Grandmother said and laughed. "PB&J? Really!" she sounded a bit frustrated. Then she said slowly, as if the men would need her to slow down in order to understand, "*Petit Bateau* and Jack."

Grandfather, John, and Jack did like the joke and laughed heartily for quite a while. "The signature food of the summer," Grandfather then declared. "We will eat them every day," he proclaimed, and everyone laughed again.

Jack really did like PB&J sandwiches, especially if they had just a bit too much jelly on them. Grandmother must have known that too. As they ate and Grandmother scrubbed the sticky peanut butter off the knife, John and Grandfather talked about the life of the cove.

"Jack," said John, "did you see the huge school of skipjacks that ran under your boat this morning? There were thousands."

Jack had not seen them and didn't know what to say. John turned to Grandfather and said, "It's a bumper crop this year. That's a good sign."

"It is," said Grandfather. "I think it's a good year for everyone. The sunfish seem to have made a comeback. I was very worried we wouldn't see them ever again. The whole cove looks so much more like it did twenty years ago. I'm amazed."

Grandmother took the sandwich plate from the table and added, "Now if we see an Indigo Bunting, we will really have a special summer."

"The other gauge will be the number of greenback turtle babies trekking down to the shore in the next few weeks," said John, referring to map turtles, which the locals called "greenback" turtles. "They should be along any day now."

"I can't wait to see them," Grandmother said with such joy in her voice that Jack even looked up at her.

Jack did not know exactly what they were talking about, but he knew they were happy and thought he should join the conversation. "Maybe we can get fishing poles and catch a bunch of fish," he interjected. "If we had a motor for *Petit Bateau*, we could go out farther and catch more."

There was a strange moment in the cabin just then. Grandfather looked down at his plate. John looked directly at Jack, and Grandmother quickly put her hand on John's arm, and said, "Jack, I'm worried that your grandfather is working too hard in the garden right now because of all the weeds."

"Kate, I'm fine, really," Grandfather said.

"I can help," said Jack.

"That would be really nice of you," said Grandmother.

"C'mon, Grandfather, let's get those weeds out of there," Jack prompted.

With that, the men rose from the table, thanked Grandmother for the lunch, and headed out.

"Al, I found the old auger post we used to use for the canoe," said John. "While you fellows weed, I'll sink it off the dock so we can tie the boat up for the night."

"Thanks, John," Grandfather replied. "That's great."

While Grandfather and Jack pulled weeds from around the radishes, Jack was still excited about the possibility of a motor for *Petit Bateau* and the chance of fishing. He asked his grandfather how fast the boat might go with a motor and what was the best bait to use for catching sunfish. Grandfather remained quiet for a while, but then finally looked at Jack and said, "Let me explain something."

Jack felt the moment strongly, as if he had said something wrong and made his grandfather angry. He stiffened his body, felt tense, and defensive.

Grandfather paused for a moment, and then started slowly. "Each early summer, the mother sunfish feels the need to build a nest for her babies. She finds a spot that she thinks will be safe, and then she swishes her tail back and forth and pushes the sand out into a perfect circle. It's amazing how perfect the circle is." He paused remembering. "At the bottom of the circle are little rocks, and she lays her eggs there. Then, a male sunfish, the one she has chosen and allowed to come near, spreads his sperm over the eggs so they will become baby sunfish."

Jack blushed. He knew that sperm was a sex word. He didn't exactly know what it meant, but he knew it had to do with making babies. Grandfather said it so openly that Jack felt that it was not the same as when his friends had said the word at school.

"Then the mother and father sunfish take turns fighting off bass and other fish that want to eat the eggs," Grandfather continued. "They spend every minute, night and day, hovering above the nest and chasing predators away by trying to bite them. Both the mother and father sunfish get skinny and tired, because they don't have enough time to find food for themselves. They sacrifice their health to make sure their babies will hatch." Then Grandfather said, "It isn't fair to dangle a hook and worm above a hungry sunfish taking care of her nest."

Jack felt uncomfortable. He had not understood how Grandfather loved the sunfish and tried to take care of them. Jack had said many things wrong, but Grandfather smiled and said, "I'm really tired of weeding for today, Skipper. Why don't you go check on your boat, and I'll finish up by watering the lettuce."

The day had been long and full. Jack felt tired when Grandmother put dinner on the table. "Jack, it's about time for a quick shower and off for bed with you. You've had a pretty big day today," she said after he had stopped eating and was sitting silently.

He was tired, but suddenly he had a very clear thought that felt right, and he said, "I'm going to practice rowing and try to find sunfish nests, like you talked about, Grandfather. I can do that in the morning, and then I want to help you with the garden in the afternoon."

"That sounds like a great plan, Jack," said Grandmother. "If you two fellows weed and water every afternoon, we're going to have a feast before you know it."

Jack smiled, felt happy, and slept well that night.

Chapter Six

Jack's plan for the following day quickly turned into the everyday routine at the lake. In fact, it was nearly a week before the schedule was broken.

Each morning, Jack set off in *Petit Bateau* to explore the cove. He always headed north, but he didn't exactly think about why he never headed south. His rowing became smooth and balanced. His arms and back became stronger, and he could row for much longer before taking a break.

When he did take a moment to slow down, he sat quietly and listened. He heard the kingfishers' rapport. He heard the ripples slapping the hull of *Petit Bateau*. He heard the splash of a bass as it chased the minnows only a few feet away from the boat, and it startled him a little.

Each day, Jack gradually heard more and saw more. He saw the clouds of skipjack minnows, and one time, a school of minnows swam right under his boat. He almost slipped as he shifted his weight to the other side to see them come out from under *Petit Bateau*. When they swam straight, they were dark green and hard to see. When they turned and rolled to one side, the sun sparkled off their silvery sides, and flashes of light lit up the water. In the garden with Grandfather later that afternoon, Jack eagerly recounted the experience of seeing the minnows flashing and rolling.

By the third day of his explorations, Jack had covered about half of the northern "half-moon" of the cove. He began to spend more time watching and listening than rowing. Then a remarkable thing happened. As if all the creatures of the cove had agreed to accept Jack as a resident of the cove, they allowed him into their world! It was like awakening to a land he had never before seen. Without any warning, Jack began to see them all.

The turtles sunned themselves on the fallen tree limbs jutting into the water. Some were very big and must have been many years old, but others were only two inches wide and struggled to pull themselves up onto a log. Jack laughed when a little one slipped off a log and tumbled back into the water. Those not able to find room on a log swam nearby with just their noses above the surface of the water. As Jack tried to come close to them, their noses sank, and through the clear water, he could see them swimming fast along the sandy bottom.

Mallard ducklings had hatched. Tiny ping-pong-ball bits of fluff, the babies swam faster than Jack thought possible for being so small, as they tried to keep up with their mother, who was busy teaching them where to find food and how to avoid predators. Jack counted the babies. Eleven "fluff balls" chased after their mother.

The muskrats stayed close to shore and swam under and around the tree roots in the shallow waters. Jack felt unsure whether he liked them or not. Their furry noses rising above the water as they swam along looked friendly, but a chill rose along Jack's spine when he saw their hairless, rat-like tails as they climbed out onto the bank.

Jack soon learned that most of the cove's "young" stayed close to the shore. The baby bass swam through the reeds in water only inches deep. The snails that left paths in the sandy bottom did not venture more than a few hundred feet from the shore. Jack liked wading in the shallow water, pulling *Petit Bateau* by the bowline behind him, and following the snails' paths to eventually find them many feet ahead still slowly pushing through the sand.

As he stood in the shallow water looking at a particularly colorful snail slowly push ahead, he felt a tap, a poke—or was it a pinch?—on his ankle. He looked down into the clear, sun-lit water and saw the sunfish coming again, back toward his ankle. "Ouch," Jack said aloud, even though the bite had not really hurt very much.

The sunfish retreated a few feet to a perfect little circle in the sand with small pebbles in the center. After a few seconds, she came back out and tried to bite Jack's ankle again. Jack smiled and laughed. He was not in any danger, and the sunfish was simply protecting her nest. He could see her sunny, yellow tummy, and he even thought her red-ringed eyes looked as mad as his mother's did when she discovered he had drawn on his bedroom wall with crayons.

"Okay, okay," he said aloud. "I'm moving on. Calm down. Not here to hurt you." With that, Jack laughed and pulled himself back into *Petit Bateau* and started to row home.

After a few days of Jack helping Grandfather weed and water the garden each afternoon, they had a hard time finding many weeds to pull. The radishes were beginning to show their red tops through the ground, and the green tomatoes started to turn red in spots. Jack noticed that instead of heading out to the garden each morning, Grandfather would come down to the lake and sit and talk with John.

Chapter Seven

During the first few afternoons of pulling weeds in the garden, Jack talked to Grandfather about the latest video games he had bought. Grandfather learned more about video games than he ever thought he would. He even decided that he might like to try one of Jack's favorites. After a few days, though, Jack wanted to talk more about the cove, the fish, the birds, and the "greenback" turtles that he had seen in the morning. When Jack told Grandfather about the sunfish biting his ankle, Grandfather laughed as loudly as Jack had ever heard him laugh.

"You have to respect her courage, don't you?" he said to Jack.

John had finished repairing the old, dock boards days ago, and he would often come sit next to the garden and talk with Jack and Grandfather. He identified the small school of black fish that Jack had seen, the ones that seemed just like little round bodies with almost no tails at all, as catfish hatchlings.

"You know, Jack," John said one afternoon, "you handle *Petit Bateau* really well. You have a natural way of rowing and feeling her. Being one with your boat is a gift. You have that."

Jack felt warm inside and smiled, but he didn't know what to say. During the next few days, John showed Jack how to tie a bowline, as well as the clove hitch that he used to tie the stern line to the auger post out from the dock. Jack learned the bowline in just a few days, but he always seemed to start the clove hitch by putting the first loop on the post backwards.

"Okay, so you're a different kid," John said to Jack and laughed. "Most people take years to learn the bowline, but they get the clove hitch right away." Jack laughed at that and knew that John was not making fun of him.

As each day passed, the wind started from the south just a bit earlier and felt a bit warmer. After a few days, the late morning sun felt hot, and Jack thought about taking off his shirt. He never liked taking off his shirt because he thought he was too skinny, but after a few hot days rowing farther up the cove, he realized that the ducks and fish would not care, and he took off his shirt and swam in the cove next to *Petit Bateau*. It felt warm and refreshing at the same time, so after that,

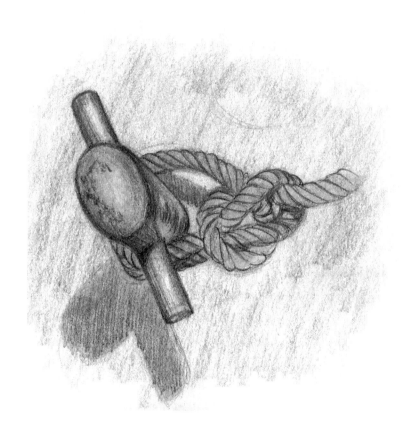

he rarely put his shirt back on except at dinner when Grandmother would insist.

The days flowed together, and Jack wasn't sure if he had been at the lake for a week or for a year. Grandfather explained that the hot and humid weather had slowed the drying of the varnish on the mast and boom but that Jack would soon sail *Petit Bateau*.

The next day, as Jack skipped down toward the dock and another morning with *Petit Bateau*, John came around the corner of the cabin and shouted down to Jack, "Not today, my friend."

Within an hour, Grandfather, Grandmother, Jack, and John were squeezed into the tiny cabin bathroom, listening as the front line of the storm hit. The wind screamed, and Jack hugged his grandmother tightly. Lightning struck an old tree a few hundred feet from the cabin, and the explosion of sound shook the cabin and everyone in it. The storm rolled, rumbled, and blew only a few frightening, intense minutes, and then a solid downpour of rain followed for an hour or more. Jack went with John to the front of the cabin to look out and was happy to see that *Petit Bateau* was still tied securely to the dock, but that she was riding lower in the water because the rain had filled her.

"You'll have some bailing to do," John said calmly.

It took Jack more than half an hour to bail all the water with a bucket and sponge. It felt longer, and he was tired when he squeezed the last of the rainwater from the sponge, but he was happy to see her floating high again.

"How did you know there was going to be a storm?" Jack asked John.

"Years of living up here and paying attention to the signals," John replied. "Several days in a row of warm winds from the south often build to a storm from the west. After living by the lake for a while, you just kind of feel these things."

The next morning, a single, sharp ray of light shone through the peaked front window of the cabin, right onto Jack's face. He grabbed another blanket from the foot of the bed and tried to hide under its warmth. The light disappeared for seconds at a time as huge, white, billowing clouds passed between the cabin and the sun. The unusual, chill, morning air inspired Jack to burrow deeply into the blankets and decide to sleep a bit longer.

"Hey, Skipper!" Grandfather shouted up to the loft. "Gotta get up, kiddo. Breakfast is almost cold."

As Jack pulled on his hoodie sweatshirt and slowly climbed down from the loft, both Grandfather and Grandmother seemed to be moving faster as they washed dishes and swept the floor. The chill in the cabin penetrated Jack's hoodie, and he shivered as he ate.

"These are the greatest days at the lake," Grandfather cheerfully began as he sat down across the table from Jack. "After a rocking, good storm, the cool, high-pressure front from the north sweeps in with crystal-clear, blue skies; puffy, white clouds; and the freshest breeze. You're going to have a great day on the water, Jack." Grandfather smiled and winked.

"I think it's cold," Jack said quietly.

Grandfather laughed and said, "Don't worry. You'll warm up soon when you start rowing up the cove against that breeze."

"Jack," said Grandmother, "keep an eye out for Indigo Buntings. I just think this summer one of us will see one."

As Jack boarded *Petit Bateau*, John and Grandfather sat on the dock and talked about the North breeze that was building. "Jack," said John, "if you feather the oars rowing upwind, it'll be a lot easier for you."

John held out his arms as if they were oars. As he pulled his arms back in toward his body, he rotated his hands to horizontal with his palms up. As he brought them forward, they were vertical again. "See?" he said. "When the oars come back through the wind, by keeping them flat, the wind can't push against them so much. It's a bit tricky at first, but you'll get it."

Jack wasn't so sure, but he said, "Okay," and pushed off from the dock. The breeze had already become fresh and strong, and Jack did feel the pressure of the wind against the oars as he pushed them back for each stroke. He tried to tilt the oars as John had shown him, and immediately the oars sliced easily through the wind. It made him smile. However, he did have trouble rotating the oars perfectly back to vertical. Sometimes they were angled too shallowly or too deeply. Jack felt as though he was learning how to row all over again as he learned to feather and row.

As he looked up the cove, Jack saw that the wind-made ripples almost had white caps on their peaks, but closer to shore, the surface of the water still shone smooth and glassy. The woods were blocking the wind and being closer to shore would keep him out of the wind and make rowing much easier. "I can look for Grandmother's birds along the shore," he said to himself, not wanting to admit that he was hiding from the wind.

On such a clear and sunny morning, Jack never thought that something bad could happen. The idea never crossed his mind. However, yesterday's storm was a good example that things can change quickly.

Chapter Eight

It's difficult to know exactly how, even in just a split second as he glanced over his shoulder and saw the mallards near the willow log, Jack knew something was wrong. Maybe it was how the ducklings huddled tightly together instead of swimming freely. Maybe it was how the mother mallard was too close to the log, her neck stretched out too high, and her beak moving but with no sound coming out. In the next second, Jack saw what his tightening stomach had already felt. A plastic fishing line was tangled around the mother mallard's neck. The babies were confused and peeping, and there was a desperate look in the mother mallard's eye.

It's also difficult to understand exactly how Jack knew instantly that he needed help to save the mallard. He needed Grandfather and John. So he didn't hesitate to turn *Petit Bateau* around and row as hard as he could back downwind.

As John and Grandfather watched Jack and *Petit Bateau* coming straight back toward the dock, they stood up, glanced at each other, and prepared to catch the dinghy as it came fast downwind onto the dock.

"The mallard," Jack said between his panting breaths. "She's caught on the log. Fisherman's line. She's choking."

There was no hesitation. "I've got my knife, Al," said John "Get in the bow, Jack." "You want to row?" John asked Grandfather.

"Yes!" Grandfather replied.

With only a few, long, powerful strokes, Grandfather had *Petit Bateau* driving through the water, leaving a strong wake behind her. Jack felt the boat surge ahead with each stroke, and through *Petit Bateau*, he felt his grandfather's strength and determination. Jack watched Grandfather feather the oars smoothly and then pull long strokes that generated deep swirls of water, like watery tornadoes, around each oar blade.

"Jack, point out the log," said John. Jack squinted in the bright light and pointed his arm directly at the log many hundreds of feet ahead.

"A bit to port, Al," said John, and Grandfather pulled slightly harder on the starboard oar, and *Petit Bateau* lined up with Jack's arm. No more than a minute later, John said, "Hold up, Al," and

Grandfather dug the oars into the water, and *Petit Bateau* came to a stop.

"She's right over there," Jack pleaded as if they had not understood and again pointed to the log. He didn't know why they had stopped short of their goal.

"Jack, take the oars," said John, and as he stepped over the starboard side into the shallow water, Grandfather simultaneously slid over the port side. *Petit Bateau* didn't roll a bit.

"I'll cut the fishing line. You hold her?" John asked Grandfather.

"Yes," Grandfather calmly replied.

"Jack," John said, while turning slowly, "the babies are going to panic. They'll want to scatter and likely head south. Row the boat in front of them and herd them together. When we free the mother, she'll head to them straight away. If any get separated, she may never find them again."

Jack understood, took the oars, and watched Grandfather and John wade toward the log. He could see the babies starting to push into each other and become frantic as the men approached. Just as John had predicted, they started to swim erratically and scatter toward the south.

It's difficult to say how much time passed. It might have been only a few minutes, but Jack's mind filled with hundreds of images that he would remember for days: Grandfather reaching out to the mallard as she flapped her wings desperately; John's knife blade catching a brief spark of sunlight as he guided it toward the fishing line; baby ducklings practically running across the water in panic.

Jack rowed to the left and stood and waved his arms at the ducklings to get them to turn back toward their mother. He rowed back to the right to cut off two babies that had gone the other way. He rowed back toward the left just in time to turn the others back again toward their mother, and then he heard the loudest quacking he had ever heard. The mother mallard was free.

Chapter Nine

Grandfather and John waded back from the log with broad smiles, and called out to Jack to come to them. Jack watched the mallard paddling furiously and using her wings almost like oars to get to her ducklings. He backed *Petit Bateau* away from the ducklings and toward Grandfather and John.

As John and Grandfather climbed into the boat, Jack moved forward to the bow and watched the mother mallard herd her babies into a tight circle and then lead them north past the log. Jack counted. One, two, three, four, five, six, seven, eight, nine, ten ... ten.

"There were eleven," Jack said almost silently. Then he turned to his grandfather and said loudly, "There were eleven!"

"What do you mean?" Grandfather asked.

"There were eleven when I counted them a few days ago," Jack replied. "Now there are only ten. I must have missed one. I didn't see it get away. I thought I had them all together." His throat tightened.

"No, no, no, Jack," Grandfather said. "You did great! I saw you rowing. You corralled them all. I know it. It's hard to count them. They move so fast. You didn't miss a one," Grandfather insisted.

John sat still for a moment, looked down into the bottom of *Petit Bateau*, and then turned her toward home. While she glided downwind, the three said nothing. Jack kept going over in his head what had happened. How had he lost the eleventh duckling? He couldn't believe one was gone. His eyes stung, and he had to look away until the mallard and her babies were out of sight.

Jack spent the afternoon up in the loft quietly playing a video game. He came down for dinner when Grandmother called him. He sat silently through most of the meal and listened while Grandmother and Grandfather talked about which vegetables were ready to be harvested from the garden. They argued a bit about the lettuce. Grandmother said that it needed another week to grow, but Grandfather thought it was ready for the first cutting. Jack thought Grandmother was right.

Grandfather finished his plate quickly and stood up. "You did great today, Jack," he said. He looked at Grandmother and added, "I'm going to check on—well, ... something ... in the shed."

As Jack and Grandmother finished their dinner, Grandmother reached across the table and took Jack's hand. "I know you're upset," she began quietly. "I just want to tell you something. If it weren't for you, none of them would be okay. You saved them. Please try to remember that." She paused and looked past Jack, through the window, toward the cove. "I used to count ducklings when I was your age. What happens, though, is that there are always fewer at the end of the summer than in the beginning. Raccoons, herons, bass, snakes—there are a lot of predators. It's nature's way. You helped them today. That's what counts." Grandmother kissed Jack on the top of his head as she headed off toward the bedroom.

Jack longed just to sleep and hide under the blankets. He would never know what had happened to the eleventh duckling, but he would always feel responsible. His stomach felt tight and upset as he pulled the blanket up under his chin.

Chapter Ten

He hid under the blankets until early the next morning when he was awakened by a loud crackling and popping sound that bounced off every wall of the cabin.

"Heavens above, Allan!" Grandmother shouted above the noise. "Why do you have to do that in the cabin?" Then, she smiled at Grandfather and walked out of the cabin, toward the lake.

Grandfather had brought *Petit Bateau*'s crisp new Dacron sail into the cabin, along with the gaff and boom to which it would be tightly roped. He shook the sail as if to lay it out flat, and the sharp crackling of the fabric made Jack want to look over the railing to watch. The dining table and the sofa had been pushed back, making an open space. There, spread out on the wooden floor, was a sparkling, white sail with a sunny-yellow number eleven in the upper corner. Grandfather pulled tangles from a white cord and looked up. "Can you give me a hand, Skipper?" he asked.

Grandfather showed Jack how to run the cord around the boom and through the sail grommets and back around the boom. In a few minutes, the sail was stretched tightly between the spars, and Grandfather announced, "Time to go sailing." He laughed and scooped up the sail and spars and nearly hit Jack with the boom as he headed out the door toward the lake.

Jack ducked and then rushed after Grandfather.

When they had walked part of the way to the dock, Jack saw that John had pulled *Petit Bateau* alongside the dock and was placing the mast through the hole in the forward seat. "Now, I'm going to let John take it from here, Skipper," Grandfather said as he handed the sail and spars over to John. Before Jack realized it, Grandfather had gone back up the dock and was heading toward the garden.

"The breeze has let up a bit, Jack," said John. "Going to be a nice first sail," he added as he laid the sail and spars across the seats. "Hop in and put the dagger board into the trunk." Jack climbed over the sail and spars, pushed them to the side, and dropped the dagger board into the slot. It went down only so far and then hit the sandy bottom. "There's a pin and a hole in the board about halfway down," John told him. "It's too shallow at the dock for the full board, but when you get out

30

toward the lake, you can pull the pin and let her down all the way." Jack liked the idea that he would be heading out toward the lake.

"Okay, my friend, pull on the halyard and raise the sail," John said, pointing to a line running up through a hole at the top of the mast and back down again. One end was tied to the gaff, and Jack pulled on the other end. As he did, the gaff, the sail, and, finally, the boom lifted off the seats and swung freely in the wind. Jack ducked under the boom as it swung about. John explained how Jack needed to wrap the line under the forward seat and then around the belaying pin that held it tight.

"Have to watch your head," John warned, laughing a little as the boom swung back and nearly grazed Jack's head.

John mounted the rudder on the transom and connected the tiller, and suddenly Jack felt as though he had never seen his boat before. *Petit Bateau* was entirely different. She had become a new boat that morning. There were ropes everywhere. There was a tiller and a rudder that swung around as the waves slapped against it. The dagger board stuck up above the center seat. The wind shook the sail, and *Petit Bateau* was no longer a quiet boat. The sail crackled and popped as the wind shook it. Jack was excited and a bit nervous.

"How about I come with you the first time, and then you take her from there?" John asked.

"Sure," Jack quickly replied.

"Okay, then, take the tiller and mainsheet, and I will cast off," John directed as he began to untie the bowline.

Jack knew that the tiller steered the boat, and he guessed that the mainsheet was the line that pulls the sail in and out. He pulled on the mainsheet until it felt tight and the boom had stopped flopping from side to side. Immediately, *Petit Bateau* lurched forward and heeled over a little. In a split second she bumped her bow hard on the dock right next to John, and the collision nearly threw Jack off his balance.

"Whoa, whoa, Skipper," said John excitedly. "Let the sail out!" Jack released the mainsheet, and the sail started to flop around again. Jack looked up at John to see if he was angry.

"So, okay," John laughed. "That's like pushing on the gas in a car. When you trim the sail in, she's going to take off. When you're at the dock, just let the sail flop around until you're ready to go."

"Sorry," Jack said loudly enough to be heard over the noise of the sail.

"No problem, Skipper," said John. "Okay. Let's go sailing," he added as he tossed the bowline into the boat and stepped softly right into the center of the boat so that she didn't roll even the slightest from his additional weight. He sat down on the floor with his back against the forward seat, each hand on a gunwale, and faced Jack. *Petit Bateau* drifted sideways away from the dock, and John said, "All right, sheet in the sail a bit and off we go."

Jack worried that he would make another mistake, so he pulled the sail in slowly and not very far. As he did, he let go of the tiller to use both hands on the mainsheet, but *Petit Bateau* started to turn back upwind toward the dock, so Jack quickly grabbed the tiller again with one hand. He instinctively pulled the mainsheet to his mouth, held it in his teeth, and then he reached out farther to pull more line in.

"You may lose some teeth doing that when it's really windy," John said with a smile. "Just pull the line to your tiller hand, and then you can grab another length of it."

Jack didn't want to pull more sail in right then because *Petit Bateau* already surged along faster than Jack had ever rowed. The forward half of the sail was still luffing and flopping, but the back half of the sail looked full and tight with the wind in it. Jack looked up at the bright, white sail with the sunny number eleven. He looked ahead at the bow and saw little splashes of water coming over the bow as *Petit Bateau* cut through the small waves. He also looked behind at the long wake fanning out in a wide "V."

There was a lot to see and watch at that moment, but as Jack turned his head back and forth, *Petit Bateau* swung upwind and the whole sail started to flop and shake again. Jack realized that he should steer her back off the wind, but as he pushed the tiller away, she turned even more upwind and the boom came swinging across.

"Ahhh! What do I do?" Jack ducked and exclaimed with a bit of a laugh. *Petit Bateau* swung all the way through the wind, and the sail on the other side filled quickly.

Jack let the mainsheet go, spun his body around, and switched hands on the tiller. With the sail shaking and flopping, *Petit Bateau* slowed nearly to a stop.

He sheeted in the line again, and *Petit Bateau* powered forward, back toward the dock. Jack pulled the tiller toward him, and she swung downwind, through the eye of the wind again, but this time the boom came slamming over hard and fast. Jack just barely ducked his head in time to avoid being hit. Meanwhile, John sat low enough in the boat that he didn't have to lower his head as the boom flew across to the other side.

"John! Geez, what do I do? Ahhh!" Jack exclaimed as he spun around again and switched hands on the tiller again, while *Petit Bateau* completed the unplanned circle.

"It's okay, Skipper," John said reassuringly. "You're fine,"

"What do you mean?" Jack laughed with some nervousness. "I'm all over the place! Here, you steer," he said to John.

"No, no," John laughed. "It just takes some getting used to."

"How do I stop spinning in circles?" Jack asked and laughed harder. *Petit Bateau*, with her sail flopping in the wind again, had slowed back to a stop.

"Well, it's kind of hard to steer and set the sail if you have no direction planned," replied John.

"Huh?" Jack responded.

John pointed nearly upwind and said, "When you head close to the wind, the sail needs to be in all the way." He moved his arm to the side and away from the wind. "When you head across the wind, the sail should be about halfway out." Then he pointed his arm downwind and said, "And when you head downwind, the sail is all the way out. It helps to keep her headed in one direction and then you can practice pulling the sail in to the right point."

Jack thought he understood and said, "Okay, so let's head out toward the lake. The wind will be coming across from the side, right?"

"Yes, that's a good way to start," replied John.

Jack pulled just enough sail in so *Petit Bateau* started to move ahead. As she gained a little speed, Jack concentrated on steering her straight. He looked behind and saw the wake coming off her transom in a straight line. They weren't moving very fast, but Jack was glad that he was steering better and not spinning in circles. His smile became more relaxed as his steering became more confident.

"You'll know when you have the sail set right when it is in just tight enough that the front part of the sail doesn't luff and flop," John said.

Jack didn't pull more sail in right away because he was still concentrating on steering smoothly. In a moment, though, he looked up at the sail and saw that only the back half was filled with wind, so he pulled the mainsheet farther in. *Petit Bateau* sped up quickly, heeled more to starboard, and Jack instinctively shifted his weight quickly to the port side of the boat that was heeling up. The sudden increase in speed and heeling scared Jack a little, so he let the mainsheet slip out through his fingers a foot or two, and *Petit Bateau* leveled and slowed.

"Cool," Jack said to himself.

For the next few minutes, Jack concentrated on steering straight ahead while trimming the sail in and out. Each time he pulled the sail in a bit farther, he felt how much he had to pull on the tiller to keep *Petit Bateau* straight on course. He got used to the increases in speed and the heeling. He smiled broadly when *Petit Bateau* surged ahead

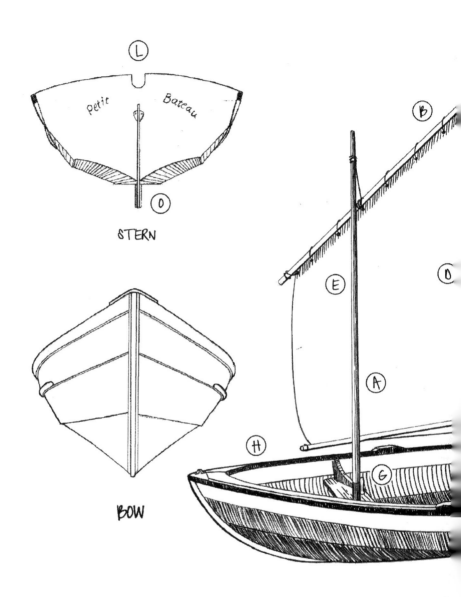

STERN

Petit Bateau

BOW

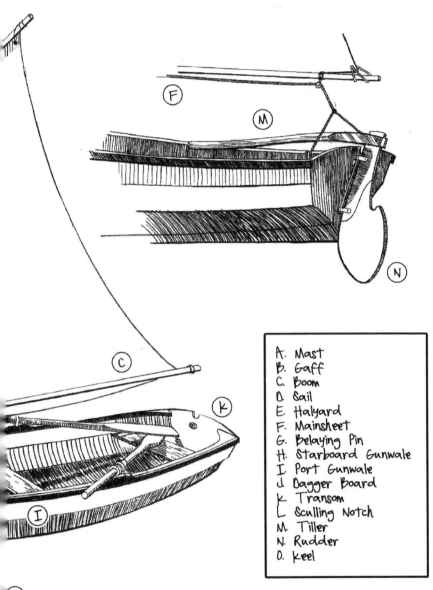

A. Mast
B. Gaff
C. Boom
D. Sail
E. Halyard
F. Mainsheet
G. Belaying Pin
H. Starboard Gunwale
I. Port Gunwale
J. Dagger Board
K. Transom
L. Sculling Notch
M. Tiller
N. Rudder
O. Keel

and the sail was full and pulling her along with power. Without luffing or flopping, the sail became quiet, and Jack's ears filled instead with the sound of wind and waves.

"Now you got her!" John said cheerfully.

"Wow, we are flying!" said Jack above the sound of water rushing under her hull and the bow slapping the small waves aside.

"So let's head up the cove now," John suggested. "Why don't we try to get to the big weed patch up by the north end?"

"Okay," Jack replied happily.

Jack knew the weed patch well and liked it. He had rowed to it several times. Short, sunny-yellow-green seaweed grew in bunches out of the sandy bottom. Narrow, little, sandy paths wound through the weeds. Jack and *Petit Bateau* had drifted over the weeds, and Jack had watched minnows darting along the sandy paths and hiding in the weedy patches. He thought that it looked like a little town with sandy roads connecting green houses and buildings.

Jack never thought again about putting a motor on the back of *Petit Bateau*. She sailed as fast as he could imagine he would ever want to go. Besides, sailing was fun! Jack shifted his weight with each puff of wind and grinned as *Petit Bateau* surged ahead in stronger puffs of wind. He trimmed the sail in and out and began to feel just when it was trimmed at the right spot. His confidence grew with each new direction they sailed.

Jack had not known that *Petit Bateau* had this whole other personality—her sailing personality. He liked it. She heeled and splashed and was noisy and fast. He also had not known that he would be able to sail a boat. He could. He liked how his hand felt gripping the smooth, varnished tiller and steering her wherever he decided to go.

"Okay, I'm serious now, Jack," said John. "You're doing really well. Do you feel it? Do you feel that sweet spot when you are right on the edge of the wind, but not too close?"

"Yeah, you can feel it. It's easy," Jack said with a grin.

Jack, John, and *Petit Bateau* sailed all over the north end of the cove. They came in close to shore where the wind shifted back and forth because the trees disrupted the flow of air. They sailed out toward the lake, almost to the edge of the cove, where the wind was steady and stronger and the waves rolled bigger. They sailed downwind and upwind and across the wind. Jack trimmed the sail in or out as he changed course, and he shifted his weight as *Petit Bateau* heeled to one side or the other. All his days of rowing *Petit Bateau* had helped prepare him for this morning of sailing. He moved confidently, his arms were strong, and he knew his boat well.

That morning, out on the clear waters of the little cove, Jack learned that sailing your own boat to a destination of your choosing feels good. He smiled and laughed and talked to John about sailing as they made their way back down to the dock. Just as they were coming into the dock, Jack said to John, "You were right. It helps to know where you're going."

John smiled and said, "Yes. It does."

Chapter Eleven

At lunch, they all ate peanut butter and jelly sandwiches for the second time that summer. "So, PB&J again, huh?" Grandfather smiled at Grandmother.

"Well," Grandmother explained, "today was another important day for PB&J. The first sail!" She clapped her hands and looked proudly at Jack. He laughed happily, with a bit of jelly on his upper lip.

"Now I know why you call him 'Skipper,' Al," said John. "He's a natural. You should see his tacks. He has a light feel on the tiller. Really remarkable."

Jack smiled, finished the other half of his sandwich, and then the whole morning's joy just flowed out of him. "She is soooo fast!" he started, dragging the "so" out a bit too long. John and Grandfather smiled, and Grandmother sat down at the table with them. "I mean, we were going downwind, and this puff came up behind and, wham!—we just flew. The bow, like, gets up out of the water, and you can hear the water rush underneath. It's so cool!"

"Isn't that a great feeling?" Grandfather remarked.

"So, going upwind is tricky," Jack said more seriously. "You have to feel when you are on the edge of the wind, and then she heels over in the puffs, and you have to get on the high side or let the sail out a bit," Jack went on. "I thought we were going to tip over a couple of times," he laughed. "I think I'm getting the hang of it, though. When we were going upwind one time, and she heeled over a bunch, I could look over the side and see the dagger board underwater," Jack continued. "Oh, and then we got too close to that shallow spot over by the weed patch and hit bottom." Jack laughed again. "John told me to pull up the board, and we just slid right back off the sand and started sailing again. I can't wait to go out again tomorrow." He paused to drink his milk.

"Tomorrow?" Grandfather spoke up. "What about this afternoon?"

"Don't you need me in the garden?" Jack asked.

"Actually, there's not much left to do in the garden, and besides, the wind is perfect today," Grandfather explained "Tomorrow there may be no wind at all," he added, and then with his arms raised above his head and a smile on his face, he commanded: "Hoist the main-sail, Skipper! I want to go sailing with you!"

"All right!" replied Jack.

Actually, there was wind the next morning, plenty of wind. The old sailors around the lake would call it a "fresh breeze," but novice sailors would call it "pretty darn windy." Jack had fallen asleep that night trying to remember all that his grandfather had taught him on their afternoon sail. The rope that pulls the sail and boom in and out is called the mainsheet. Turning the bow through the eye of the wind sailing up-wind is called a tack, but turning the boat through the eye of the wind going downwind is called a jibe. When tacking, the boom gradually swings over as the boat comes around, but the boom slams over in a jibe, and the sailor has to keep his head down.

Jack heard the "fresh breeze" in the trees around the cabin as he awakened, and as his eyes barely opened, he smiled and thought: Y*ay! There is wind today!*

He practically slid down the loft ladder and ran into the kitchen where, as usual, Grandfather was cooking the morning breakfast. "Whoa, Skipper!" Grandfather proclaimed. "What's the rush? I haven't even started the eggs yet."

"That's okay," Jack said. "Thanks. I'm not that hungry," he declared as he grabbed a piece of toast and jelly off the counter and shoved the wooden screen door open. He stopped himself, just as the rusty spring on the screen door slammed it back shut with a bang. He looked back through the screen toward Grandfather and said, "Sorry. I just want to go sailing while the wind is up."

"Understood," Grandfather replied with a smile. "Go get 'em, Skipper."

As he ran down toward the dock, Jack saw that the breeze had brought energy to the cove with white-capped waves rolling and birds dancing on the fast, shifting currents of wind. He grinned and thought: *This is going to be great!*

John was already on the dock and leaning over into *Petit Bateau*. As Jack came out onto the dock, he could see that John was tying a rope around the forward seat. The other end was already tied to a rubber bucket.

"What's that for?" Jack asked.

"Oh, hey, Jack," John said. "I thought you would be eager to set off today. I just have to reef the sail for you, and you can head out."

"What's a reef?" Jack asked.

"Well," John began to explain, "when the wind blows this much, it's a good idea to shorten the sail a bit. You roll the bottom few inches of sail up to those little ropes in the sail, tie them, and then the sail isn't as big, and you have less power."

"Won't she go slower?" Jack asked.

"Well, yes, that's kind of the point," John said and laughed.

Jack thought for a moment. He wanted to go fast, but he didn't want to upset John. "Can I reef the sail later if I'm going too fast?"

John paused and then said, "Well, it's harder to do out on the water. You have to lower the sail. I guess you could come back in, and then I could help you."

"Okay, that sounds good!" Jack replied, as he leapt off the dock and into *Petit Bateau*.

As Jack raised the sail, the crisp Dacron snapped and crackled more loudly than ever in the strong wind. Jack had to shout to John on the dock to tell him he was ready to cast off. John didn't respond right away. Instead, he paused and looked at Jack, almost as if he were sizing him up, and then said clearly and loudly, "Put on the life jacket."

Jack didn't question John and did as he was told.

John untied the bowline and tossed it into *Petit Bateau* as Jack sheeted in the sail and turned her across the wind and out toward the open lake. Just as Jack passed by the end of the dock, John shouted, "Keep looking upwind for the dark-green, wind patches coming down at you!"

Jack wasn't able to respond to John because he was already realizing that this breeze was going to be a handful. He had to concentrate on balancing the boat, sheeting in the sail, and steering through the waves. *Petit Bateau* felt strong and solid, but she was also light and rolled with each gust of wind and surged ahead faster than Jack had ever experienced in *Petit Bateau*.

Jack yelled, "Wahoo!" as spray sheered away from the bow and arced back into the boat. He knew from yesterday that the fastest point of sail was heading downwind, so he wanted to sail upwind first, as far up north as he could, so he would have a long, fun ride downwind. He sat high up on the windward rail, toes tucked under the center seat to keep his balance, and responded to each fresh gust of wind by steering higher or quickly letting the sail out a bit to keep *Petit Bateau* from heeling too much.

He had to adjust sail and steering faster than he had done before. He did remember what John had said about looking upwind for dark-green patches of water, and he saw them coming down the lake in streaks. The little ripples inside the dark-green puffs were sharp, quick, and almost violent. The dark water was where the wind was the strongest.

After a few minutes of sailing on a port tack, Jack's left hand started to get sore from holding onto the mainsheet, so he tacked over onto starboard and almost didn't slide to the other side of the boat fast enough. *Petit Bateau* heeled over more than ever before, and Jack saw a bit of water spill over her lower gunwale and into the bottom of the boat. Jack released the mainsheet entirely, and *Petit Bateau* rolled back upright, her sail shaking, flopping, and crackling in the wind.

"Wow!" Jack said aloud and laughed as he sheeted in again, and *Petit Bateau* took off on a port tack, climbing upwind with the rail down and Jack balancing and adjusting the sail and his weight with each oncoming gust of wind.

After he had eased out the sail during a big puff, he pulled the mainsheet back by holding it in his teeth so he could reach out and grab the line again and pull it in tighter. He remembered what John had said when he saw Jack do that yesterday, but Jack was too busy trying to keep *Petit Bateau* upright, and using his teeth seemed far more efficient in these windy conditions.

One solid, dark-green wind patch hit *Petit Bateau* especially hard, and even though Jack released the mainsheet as fast as he could, the boat heeled hard over. Jack's heart skipped several beats. The back end of the boom dragged in the water.

Jack thought: *That was a close one!*

He did remember, however, another important sailing lesson that Grandfather had told him yesterday: "If you need to stop for a minute and get things under control, just let out the sail and keep her pointed slightly across the wind."

Jack's right hand stung from holding onto the mainsheet, and he let out the sail all the way, turned slightly off the wind, and *Petit Bateau* slowed nearly to a stop. Even with the sail all the way out, shaking and crackling loudly, *Petit Bateau* heeled over a bit with each puff, and Jack still had to sit on the high-side rail to balance her.

He didn't rest for long, though, because he couldn't wait to head back downwind and feel the power of the wind at his back. He sheeted the sail in, and as *Petit Bateau* accelerated, he turned her downwind, eased the sail out, and shifted his weight back toward the center of the boat. Instantly, her bow rose up on top of the waves, spray came off both sides, and she simply soared.

Jack had thought the downwind run would be easier than sailing upwind, but he had to adjust his weight even faster and steer even more dramatically as *Petit Bateau* surged ahead with each gust coming at her from behind. *Petit Bateau* rolled from side to side, and Jack had to concentrate hard on steering and balancing. His right hand gripped the tiller tightly. He held onto both the port rail and the mainsheet with his left hand, while crouching mostly in the center of the boat but constantly balancing left and right as she rolled.

With one strong, dark-green puff of water that came up from behind, *Petit Bateau* lifted nearly all her front half out of the water and planed with spray coming off her midsection as if she were a powerboat. Jack simply yelled, "Ahhhh!" With his eyes fixed on the bow, his chest filled with a rush of joy and tightness too, *Petit Bateau* bounced over the backs of the waves rolling down the cove.

Chapter Twelve

If Jack had remembered all that his grandfather and John had shared with him yesterday, he would have remembered that jibing in strong winds is about the most difficult maneuver a small-boat sailor can tackle. He didn't remember that piece of advice, however, when he decided that he was getting out too far and too close to the edge of the big lake where the large waves were churning dark green and foaming white. He jibed *Petit Bateau* through the eye of the wind just as a strong puff came up from behind. When the boom slammed across to the other side, Jack was quick enough to duck and protect his head, but he wasn't quick enough to balance all the energy that had instantly shifted from one side to the other. *Petit Bateau* heeled drastically to port.

Everything for the next few seconds seemed to play out in slow motion. Jack saw everything as it was happening in drawn-out time, like a movie slowed down to a crawl.

He let go of the tiller and mainsheet and rolled stomach-over onto the high-side gunwale. He looked back. The end of the boom dragged through the water and made its own small wake cutting through the water. The lower gunwale sank below the dark-green water and a thick, dark flood rolled into the boat. *Petit Bateau* slowed and then stopped entirely, with her bow having turned back toward the wind. The mast rolled to horizontal and made a splash as it slapped onto the water. Jack felt his boat beginning to capsize, so he slid over the rail and landed on the dagger board that was now lying flat on top of the water. He stood up on the slippery, dagger board, held onto the gunwale, and looked at his half-sunken boat wallowing in the waves.

Time returned to normal speed. Jack didn't really think about what he was doing. He didn't stop to make a plan or weigh options. He didn't feel fear or excitement. He just reacted and did what needed to be done. He had seen other small sailboats capsize out on the lake, and he knew that a boat could be righted. He had seen how a skipper had stood on the dagger board, leaned back over the water, and pulled on the upper gunwale. He did the same, and slowly, far slower than Jack wanted, *Petit Bateau* began to roll back up, still filled to her gunwales with water.

Her mast came out of the water first, and the sail gradually spilled its load of water and began to shake off a shower of spray as it came up into the wind again. *Petit Bateau* pulled ahead a little and turned a bit farther upwind as she righted. As her mast came near vertical, Jack slipped back inside and swam in all the water sloshing around inside her.

He felt a brief moment of success, when, to his surprise, *Petit Bateau* again began to roll to port and her load of water shifted to that side, and, as Jack clung helplessly to the upper gunwale, she capsized again, her mast slapping the water even harder.

Jack realized that he had to lower the sail so he could keep her up. Being nearly submerged, *Petit Bateau* had almost no stability, and the sail, heavy with water, easily dragged her over in the strong wind.

As he stood again on the dagger board, leaned as far back as he could again, and pulled on the rail, he thought about how fast he would have to untie the halyard and get the sail down before she rolled over another time. As she came back to vertical, Jack slid inside and straight to the halyard. He un-cleated the halyard from the belaying pin, and the sail dropped quickly with the boom banging on the seats as it fell.

The next few seconds again felt much longer to Jack than they actually were. He had lowered the sail as fast as possible, but *Petit Bateau* had already started to roll back over. He flung himself onto the rising starboard side, clung there, and hoped that she would stop heeling over. She was about half way over when Jack's small weight finally counterbalanced her roll, and she began to come back up. Jack took a deep breath of relief.

Chapter Thirteen

That night, at the dinner table, he was able to put each of the day's events together: the brisk breeze, John having suggested reefing the sail, and the bucket. "He knew, didn't he?" Jack said to Grandfather.

"Well, I suppose he thought there was a pretty good chance," Grandfather replied. "John's a smart fellow and a good sailor."

His first bucketfull of water had been so heavy that Jack was barely able to lift it over the gunwale. He took much smaller loads of water after that but worked as fast as he could. Waves still tossed water into the boat, but soon Jack saw both gunwales rise an inch or two above the waves, and he knew he was going to keep her upright from that point on.

Bailing a nearly full dinghy with only a bucket is usually not much fun and certainly hard work, but Jack rejoiced as each inch of water went back out into the cove and *Petit Bateau* rose an inch higher. It may have taken twenty minutes or more of hard bailing, but as Jack's arms and back began to give out, *Petit Bateau* came back on top of the water with only a couple of inches still sloshing around in her hull.

"I wasn't going to raise the sail all the way up again. That was for sure," Jack laughed as he explained to his grandparents. "I didn't have the oars, so I figured that I could raise the sail up just a bit, sorta like the reef thing John told me about. That way, I could get her moving and head back to the dock."

"Exactly! Good job, Skipper. That worked, didn't it?" Grandfather clapped his hands together.

With the sail raised only a few feet and the boom still tucked into the boat, *Petit Bateau* began to make forward progress slowly. Jack had his sights set on the dock across the cove and steered straight for it. Before Jack really had had time to gather all his thoughts about what he had just been through, *Petit Bateau* was in John's strong arms alongside the dock.

Grandmother stood up from the dinner table and took Grandfather's plate toward the kitchen. "The lake can be dangerous, Jack," she said rather seriously. Jack looked at her back as she rinsed off the plate. "It's time for bed for all of us, I should think." As she kissed him goodnight on the forehead, she added, "You did well, honey," and she went to the bedroom.

Grandfather and Jack sat at the table for a little while longer. "Is she mad at me?" Jack asked.

"No. She was worried about you. That's all," Grandfather said kindly.

"I'm sorry," Jack said. "I didn't mean to capsize."

Grandfather laughed and said, "Of course not, Jack. Besides, I had my share of upside down moments when I was learning to sail." He laughed again and said, "It's part of the fun. You did well. Really."

As he lay in bed that night, Jack went through all the moments of the day. His head buzzed with images of wind, water, and *Petit Bateau*. Eventually, he was able to roll over and fall asleep after he had decided that he would become the best sailor ever and learn all he could from John and Grandfather.

He would have to wait to practice his sailing skills for a while, however. As the sun rose on the cove the next morning, the air was still, warm, and heavy. The chatter and scolding of nesting season was waning, and the cove was quiet, as the orange, morning sun gradually burned off the heavy dew on the dock and *Petit Bateau*'s seats.

When Jack came down to breakfast in only his swim trunks, he was already hot and felt the stillness of the air—even in the cabin. There was something else different that morning, not just the weather. He didn't smell bacon or eggs cooking. As he walked into the kitchen, Grandmother stood stirring a pot on the stove, and Grandfather wasn't even in the cabin.

"Morning, honey," Grandmother said. "Breakfast is nearly ready. Sit down."

"Where's Grandfather?" Jack couldn't help asking.

"Oh, I don't know, dear," Grandmother responded. "I'm sure he and John are off planning some big project. So, I cooked you some oatmeal this morning. You guys need to lay off the eggs for a while."

As Jack looked out the window and saw the glassy, flat, windless water of the cove, he said, "Darn!"

"Excuse me?" Grandmother said sharply.

"Oh, no, sorry, Grandmother," Jack replied quickly. "There's no wind today. That's what I meant," he explained, although he wasn't very interested in oatmeal either.

Bruce Holaday

"Well, I know you were excited to go sailing again today," she said as she placed the bowl of oatmeal in front of him and a little bowl of brown sugar next to it. Jack looked down at the oatmeal and thought that he would need all the brown sugar. "I know it's not the same as actually sailing, but your grandfather learned a lot about sailing a boat by reading," she said as she walked across the room to the bookshelf by the fireplace and pulled a hardback book from it. "I think you may like it," she said and set it down on the table next to Jack.

As he scooped several spoonfuls of brown sugar onto the oatmeal, he read the title: *Piloting, Seamanship and Small Boat Handling.*[1] He opened it and was glad to see there were lots of illustrations. On several pages were drawings of different sail patterns for boats. He read their names: sloop, cat, lateen, lug-sail.

"Hey, Grandmother, *Petit Bateau* is a lug-sail," he announced.

"Uh huh, she is," Grandmother replied.

Another illustration labeled all the parts of a small sailboat. He read gunwales, rudder, tiller, thwart, and mainsheet. Then he saw that the half circle cutout of the top of the transom was labeled sculling notch. He hadn't really thought about the cutout in the transom, why it was there, or what it was for.

"What's sculling?" he asked.

Grandmother laughed and said, "Well, some people think it's a viable means of propulsion, but I can tell you, it certainly isn't. I never could get the hang of it." She laughed again and took Jack's empty oatmeal bowl over to the sink.

Jack pushed open the screen door, and as he walked slowly down to the dock, he flipped though the book's pages looking for "sculling." Through the front window, Grandmother watched him walk all the way down to the dock before she went looking for John and Grandfather.

John had hung the wet sail and spars up in the shed to dry overnight, and he had put the oars back into *Petit Bateau*. Jack sat on the center seat and scanned through the pages of the book trying to find an explanation of sculling. Eventually, he went to the index, ran his finger down to the "s" section and found sculling on page 448.

The illustration showed a man sitting on the center seat of a rowboat, facing toward the back of the boat, holding the handle of a single oar with both hands, the oar leather in the notch in the transom, and

---

[1]Charles F. Chapman, *Piloting, Seamanship and Small Boat Handling: A Complete Illustrated Course on the Operation of Small Boats, 1967-68 edition: Volume V—Motor Boating's Ideal Series* (New York: Motor Boating [The Hearst Corporation], 1967).

the blade of the oar in the water out behind the back of the boat. The drawing had curving arrows around the man's hands, but Jack wasn't sure what they meant, so he read the two pages that described how to scull a small boat.

He learned that the arrows didn't simply mean to push the oar back and forth from side to side. Instead, sculling demanded that the skipper twist his hands from one side to the other as he also pushed the oar from side to side. Eager to try the technique, Jack untied *Petit Bateau* and pushed her away from the dock.

Chapter Fourteen

The cove was very different that morning. Jack was too interested in learning how to scull right then, but if he had taken a moment to look around, he would have seen that the surface of the water was nearly as flat and shiny as glass. Not a breath of wind stirred the surface. The sky wasn't cloudy, exactly, but the sun shone dim as if through the smog of a big city. Heaviness in the air made breathing a little more difficult, and the humid heat of the day made the oar handle feel damp and slick.

At first, Jack simply moved the single oar from side to side, and *Petit Bateau* did move ahead a little but not very much. He then twisted his wrists as he moved the oar from side to side. As he did so, the oar dug deeper into the water, and he had to tighten the muscles in his arms to keep the oar at an even height. With each side-to-side movement, he fought the oar from digging too far into the water, and *Petit Bateau* responded by gaining a little forward speed.

Jack often wanted things to be easy and fast, but he was learning that those things that are easy and fast are often not very satisfying in the long run. Learning how to row, sail, and scull a small boat isn't easy or fast, but Jack remembered that Grandmother hadn't "gotten the hang" of sculling, and knowing that, for some reason, made him more determined to learn how.

Learning how to row takes time because you have to train the muscles of the arms and back. Only after hours of rowing did Jack row steadily, smoothly, and with less effort. He had certainly learned yesterday that sailing a small boat in strong winds would take a long time to master. Today, he took the time, a couple of hours or more, to wrestle with this single oar hanging off the back of *Petit Bateau* and to learn how to scull.

Eventually, with focused concentration, he was able to twist and push the oar from side to side smoothly and strongly enough to gain a bit of forward speed. *Petit Bateau* did not move quickly under a single-sculled oar, but she did, in time, cover some distance. Jack's arms, wrists, and hands became sore, and as he stopped sculling to rest, *Petit Bateau* glided quietly to a stop on the flat water.

Jack looked up and realized that he didn't actually know quite where he was. He had pushed off from the dock, focused on learning how to scull, and had not even thought about which direction he had taken. His single oar sculling had pushed *Petit Bateau* down the cove toward the southern end. He could barely see the dock back up the cove, and he looked around to see a very different looking cove than the one he had become used to seeing.

The tall, sturdy oak trees that lined the shore of the northern half of the cove were gone, and instead, he saw short sumac trees clustered in mounds with their bright red seed pods poking above the green leaves. Tall cattail reeds hid the banks of the cove and grew far out into the shallow water. A black bird with a splash of crimson on each wing clung to the brown, tubular seed pods of the cattails. It called a loud "breeee," as it saw Jack floating near and flew back into the reeds. Farther toward the deep corner of the south cove, Jack could make out a floating "rug" of water lilies on the surface. A Great Blue Heron stood behind, his long sharp beak pointed straight at Jack.

Jack looked over the side of his boat and couldn't see the soft brown sand on the bottom that he was used to seeing. Instead, the water had turned black and hid its depth. Jack stood up and poked his oar down into the water. He felt the oar sink into soft mud a couple of feet below the surface, and when he pulled it back out of the water, the end was coated, sticky, and black. He swished the oar back and forth through the dark water, and the mud washed off. He sat down on the seat, grabbed both oars, inserted them into the oarlocks, turned *Petit Bateau* around, and rowed strongly back up the cove toward home.

Chapter Fifteen

"Why is the water so black and dark down there?" Jack asked.

"It isn't really," Grandfather said as they sat down to dinner that evening. "The bottom is mucky, and sunlight doesn't reflect off it. The mud makes the water look black."

"Why is it swampy down there?" Jack continued.

"The water for the big lake comes from underground springs deep out in the lake," Grandfather explained. "All that water has to go somewhere, and it heads toward the south end of the cove. Behind the water lilies is a small outlet creek that twists and winds for miles through reeds and swamp and eventually empties into the river way down the road."

"Allan," Grandmother suddenly said as she stopped eating and looked at her husband.

Grandfather didn't look at her but kept his eyes on Jack across the table. "It's another part of the cove that you may at some point want to explore," Grandfather told Jack. "But it can wait for another summer. Besides, you will want to go sailing tomorrow. Although John doesn't think there will be any wind again tomorrow, he has been known to be wrong. Well, maybe once or twice," he concluded and laughed softly.

John wasn't wrong. As another hazy sun slowly rose the next morning, the cove again sat still and heavy with heat and dew. Jack came down from the loft and smelled another pot of oatmeal on the stove and saw a glass of orange juice on the counter next to the stove. He looked around and then heard voices out behind the cabin near the garden. He peeked through the back screen door and saw Grandmother, Grandfather, and John looking at the garden and arguing playfully about which vegetables were ready for harvesting or not.

It was an impulse. He never could have explained why, but Jack gulped down the orange juice and ran out the front screen door, making sure that it didn't slam shut. In a minute, he had untied *Petit Bateau* and was rowing south. As he came near the water lilies, he let *Petit Bateau* drift into them, and their stiff leaves slowed her to a stop. He heard them scraping softly against her hull. Again, a black bird with a crimson wing patch called "breee" from the cattails, and as Jack looked over his shoulder, he saw another, or maybe the same, Great Blue Heron standing, this time in a small gap between the reeds.

"That must be where the creek starts," Jack said softly.

Rowing through water lilies is not easy. *Petit Bateau* rowed heavily as the leaves clung to her sides. Jack's oars stuck under the leaves, and he had to push down harder to pull the oars back up to the surface. He had gone about halfway toward the opening in the reeds when a few feet to his right, the water lilies jerked and thrashed as if a hand had brushed harshly across them. Jack knew that something under the water had shaken the lilies, and he froze for a moment trying to decide what it had been. He imagined that it had been a large fish, but he was not sure.

As he pushed *Petit Bateau* close to the opening in the reeds, the Great Blue Heron sounded "craaack" and lifted up with only a few powerful strokes of his wings and then glided down deeper into the swamp ahead. Jack had been right. The opening in the reeds was the mouth of the creek where the water from the lake made its way down toward the river miles away.

As her bow passed into the creek, *Petit Bateau* and Jack felt something they had not felt before: a current. Moving water was pulling them into the creek without effort. Jack raised the oars out of the dark water and allowed *Petit Bateau* to be pulled by the current into the opening of the creek, cattails brushing along both sides of her hull.

The creek was only slightly wider than the narrow opening that Jack had just scraped through, so Jack had to keep the oars close alongside the boat to keep them from sticking in the muddy banks and tall reeds that hung out over the water. He looked ahead over his shoulder and saw the Great Blue Heron at the point where the creek took a sharp turn to the left. Again, the tall, skinny bird sounded, "craaack" and flew down the creek and out of sight.

Jack didn't know why he was there, in this dark, muddy creek with a hot, hazy sun building above him. He understood that Grandfather and John had explored the same creek years ago, and it was probably okay. But the current kept pulling him farther down the winding creek, and he had not told anyone where he was going that morning. His stomach tightened. As *Petit Bateau* came around the bend, again, the Great Blue Heron, a hundred yards down the creek at the next bend toward the right, stood in the muddy water. Jack had barely seen the bird when he noticed to his right a dinner-plate-sized softshell turtle

slither from the muddy bank down into the dark water of the creek. Jack's stomach tightened even more. Softshell turtles are not like the "greenback" turtles in the north cove. Their shells are a yellowish brown and are slick like the skin of a snake. Their noses are sharp pointed, and their black eyes are set back. Jack couldn't see which way the softshell turtle had swum because the water was so dark. He sat still in his boat and let the current pull him deeper down the creek.

As Jack came closer to the Great Blue Heron, again it sounded, "craaack," and flew out of sight to the right this time, around the next bend in the creek. As *Petit Bateau* drifted around the right bend, Jack's nose filled with the smell of rotting flesh. He scrunched up his nose and squinted his eyes.

There, right after the bend, on the muddy bank, a bloated corpse of an opossum or maybe a raccoon rotted in the humid heat. Jack couldn't be sure which: the fur was gray and stood up, but the body had lost its shape and appeared to be simply rounded and full. Jack pinched his nose and held his breath as *Petit Bateau* swung around the bend and down farther into the deep swamp. A brief moment of regret crossed Jack's mind, but it was replaced again by seeing the Great Blue Heron watching him from the next bend.

Jack had seen little garden snakes before, and they had surprised him, but what he saw next shocked him and his chest tightened. He held his breath. A four-foot-long snake with shiny, black skin wriggled through the dark, soft mud of the bank. It slid silently into the still, black water. As it swam, swirling currents of water outlined its long, undulating body hidden beneath the black water. Its head stretched up several inches above the surface. Its dark-yellow eyes stared at Jack as it swam downstream toward the Great Blue Heron.

Jack had no further desire to follow the Great Blue Heron down the creek. The tension in his chest gradually released, and he heaved in a deep breath of the stagnant humid air. He pulled hard on the starboard oar and pushed as hard on the port oar. *Petit Bateau* swung around, her bow just skimming past the muddy bank. As *Petit Bateau* pointed back up the creek, Jack pulled hard against the current. He rowed with oars often sticking into the muddy banks on each side, and just as often he had to take only half strokes where the creek was narrowest. Although his body faced downstream, he looked over his shoulder constantly, back toward the cove, and rowed *Petit Bateau* around each bend and toward the tight opening into the cove. *Petit Bateau* responded to Jack's desire to reach the cove and glided with each stroke. Jack and *Petit Bateau* moved as one.

Jack had not considered that rowing back upstream against the current would be a challenge. His arms and back began to ache just as he pushed his way back through the mouth of the creek and into the water lilies. He could have rested for a moment among the water lilies, where the current barely pulled on *Petit Bateau*, but Jack had had enough of the south cove for now. He rowed powerfully through the water lilies even though his arms and back ached.

Chapter Sixteen

"Jack," Grandmother sounded stern, but then she paused, and Jack knew she was making an effort not to sound angry. "Honey," she said slowly and clearly, "we weren't sure where you were this morning." She paused again. "I was a bit worried where you had gone."

Grandfather sat quietly across from Jack as they ate lunch.

Jack didn't tell his grandparents about rowing south and being pulled into the creek. He didn't tell them about the Great Blue Heron, the rotting opossum or raccoon, the snake, or the muddy water. He ate his lunch slowly and kept his head down.

Finally, Grandfather broke the silence and said, "Jack, the sail has finally dried in this humidity. Let's go roll it up and figure out how to store it better in the shed. I'm thinking we need to suspend it from the rafters with rope."

The next morning, the glassy, still water of the cove shone in the brightening sun with a few, small patches of light breeze that disappeared as quickly as they appeared. There would be no sailing again today, so Jack joined John and Grandfather on the dock for most of the morning. They waited for the wind and talked about sailing, but the wind never came up.

At lunch, Grandmother said, "Sorry there's no wind again today, Jack, but that's Mother Nature for you. Anyway, we have a very busy afternoon getting ready for your going-away feast tonight."

Jack didn't understand what she meant about a feast or what she meant about going away. "What do you mean, going away?" he asked.

Grandfather spoke up and with a laugh said, "That's lake life for you. The days just run together. Time disappears." After a pause, he went on, "Your parents are coming tomorrow to pick you up. They'll be here for lunch."

Jack was stunned. He stared straight ahead without seeing because his mind filled with conflicting thoughts. He really had lost track of the days. He could not tell if it was Thursday or Friday. He thought about seeing his parents and that made him feel good. Then he thought about all the other voyages he had planned to make with *Petit Bateau* and that made him sad.

He stared at the table for a minute without saying a word. Grandmother came up right next to him and rested her hand on his shoulder. "Now, Jack," she said. "The vegetables are still pretty small, but the tiny ones taste better anyway. We have a lot of harvesting to do, so let's get hopping." She smiled down at him, and then to John and Grandfather she said with excitement in her voice, "C'mon fellas. We have work to do."

They all cheered and laughed when Jack pulled the first carrot from the ground. It was nearly six inches long and a beautiful deep orange. "Wow, Skipper, that's huge for this time of year!" laughed Grandfather.

They cut lettuce, pulled radishes and carrots, found a few good-sized zucchini hiding under the leaves, and cheered each other on as they worked. Green beans, tomatoes, and a few small cucumbers ended up in the wicker baskets and then the kitchen sink to be washed and sliced.

Jack helped Grandfather light the charcoal grill, and soon the smell of freshly cooked hamburgers filled the evening air. John said that he really should be getting home, but Grandmother insisted he stay for dinner. "John, really, you need to join us. It's not every day we get to taste the first harvest. You sit down at the table right now," she insisted.

Over dinner, Grandfather and Grandmother told stories about the first time Jack came up to the lake when he was very little. They told the story of how Jack slipped off the dock and that he refused to go near the dock for the rest of the weekend. They all laughed, even Jack.

Grandmother was right. The first harvest tastes the best. As John helped Grandmother clear the table, Grandfather said to Jack, "There's a good chance that we'll have a nice breeze in the morning. You'll get one more sail in before you have to go, Skipper."

A little while later, Jack was already in bed and began to think about his last morning at the lake. He remembered seeing *Petit Bateau* for the first time as clearly as he remembered her yesterday. He thought about what would be the best morning he could possibly have with his boat, and soon a smile came across his face, and he rolled over and went to sleep.

The breeze did come back on Jack's last morning at the lake, and the sun shone brilliantly off the streaks of shining ripples pushed down the cove by the freshening breeze. Summer had matured, and the sunfish were leaving their nests. The baby turtles had grown to at least three inches wide and swam almost as fast as their parents could. Many of the bass and bluegills had left the cove and ventured out farther into the big lake. The sun rose a bit later and went to bed a bit earlier. The cycle of the seasons steadily progressed.

As Jack ran out onto the dock, he greeted John with a wide smile and a cheerful, "Hey, John!"

"Hi, Skipper," said John. "So, do you want me to help you rig the sail?"

Jack paused just briefly and then replied, "I think I'm going to row up the shore of the cove today. Okay?"

John looked at Jack quietly, thought for a second, and said, "Yes, I think that would be good."

"Uh, John?" Jack asked.

"Yes?" His mentor replied.

"Could I borrow your pocket knife?" Jack requested.

"What do you…" John started but then stopped himself and took a second to look at Jack squarely. "Sure." He paused a moment longer and added, "We don't need any amputated fingers on your last morning at the lake, now, do we?"

Jack laughed and said, "I'll be careful. Promise."

The tiny stretch of sandy beach was farther up the cove than Jack had remembered. He rowed past the willow log and inside the weed patch, and finally he saw the small opening in the woods and the soft, brown, sandy beach. Although only a few feet wide, the beach held a treasure trove of small driftwood. Jack had stopped here several times before and knew that here he could find what he was looking for.

He dragged the bow of *Petit Bateau* up onto the sand and began searching for just the right piece of driftwood. In minutes he had found it. About six inches long, bleached white by the sun, and smoothed by the sand, wind, and water, the small piece of driftwood was perfect.

He sat down on the little beach, took John's knife from out of his swim trunk's pocket and began to carve the driftwood. He stopped every so often and looked at *Petit Bateau* next to him, then back at the driftwood, and then whittled little pieces away. He held the driftwood up to the light and turned it from side to side and then carved more little pieces away. After more than an hour of work, he held up his creation one last time and saw that it had turned out even better than he had hoped. He smiled and started to stand up when he heard it: low, soft quacking coming up the shoreline.

Only one mallard family grew up in the cove that summer. Jack knew that. His stomach tightened as they came within view. Mother mallard was out front, as always, but the ducklings roamed wider from her than Jack had remembered. They had grown. Nearly six inches long, the ducklings looked long, skinny, and awkward with patches of fluff mixed together with young feathers. Their voices sounded less like peeps and more like high-pitched quacks. They swam with more confidence and ventured away from their mother frequently. They were fast and strong paddlers. Like little motorboats, they pushed through small waves with ease, their rounded chests throwing up miniature bow waves. They pecked at each other, play fought, and quacked constantly.

Jack simply could not help himself. He counted. One, two, three, four, five, six, seven, eight, nine ... ten. He slowly stood up straight, and the mallards finally saw him, and with a burst of quacking, paddling, and tiny wings flapping scooted out from the shoreline a few feet away from Jack. They calmed down quickly and kept swimming north past the tiny beach.

Chapter Seventeen

Jack was late getting back to the dock, and his family had already arrived. Anna was sunbathing on the end of the dock. She had lain down on a towel and wore her swimsuit. Jack smiled to himself and let *Petit Bateau* glide silently close to the dock. When he was only a few feet away, he slapped the starboard oar against the water and sent a shower of spray up and all over Anna.

"You little brat!" she shouted.

Jack laughed for a bit too long, but then made up with Anna and gave her a ride in *Petit Bateau*. He even let her row for a while, although he kept criticizing how she let the oars enter the water either too shallowly or too deeply.

When Anna went up to the cabin, John came down to the dock and said to Jack, "Well?"

Jack smiled and replied by pulling the miniature driftwood *Petit Bateau* from his trunks. He held it out to John who took it and held it up and turned it around from side to side. "He will love it," said John. They tied *Petit Bateau* to the dock and sternpost, and then started to walk up the dock toward the cabin. John stopped and turned to Jack. "There's something else, isn't there? I feel it."

Jack smiled up at John and then looked up the lake toward where he had seen the mallards. He reached out and took hold of John's hand. John was a bit startled but didn't pull away. Jack looked up at John and said, "They're okay." He paused a moment and added, "They're going to be fine. They're getting really strong."

John simply nodded, gazed up toward the north end of the cove and smiled. Together, Jack and John headed up to the cabin.

Lunch was noisy, as everyone wanted to share stories of the past few weeks. Jack's parents complained about the moving company and how the dining table had been damaged. Anna went on and on and on about which horse she liked the best and how she had won two ribbons in dressage. Jack jumped in when he could and told about sailing with Grandfather and John.

As his parents packed up his things into the car, Jack stayed in the cabin and helped Grandmother finish washing the dishes. When they were finally alone, he stopped drying the plate in his hand, looked up at his grandmother and asked, "They're purple, right?"

"Honey, what are you talking about?" Grandmother asked.

"Your birds, the ink-ke-go birds," Jack replied.

"Jack," she looked at him with narrow eyes, "don't you dare tease your grandmother," she said seriously.

She walked with determination over to the bookcase by the fireplace, pulled a book from the shelf, flipped through several pages and then, with her hand covering the names, showed Jack a page with several pictures of birds. With no hesitation, he put his finger right onto the picture of an Indigo Bunting.

Grandmother sighed and just shook her head.

Jack said, "I think they like the woods, but they also like being down close to the water. I saw one at the little beach today. I didn't know it was one of your birds, but I kinda thought it might be."

Grandmother laughed aloud and hugged Jack a bit too hard. "Yes, that's exactly right! They like the dense woods but want to be near the water." She laughed and gave Jack another hug. "You are our lucky treasure, Jack."

With the car loaded and Anna still talking about her horse, Jack's parents waved for him to get in. Grandfather, Grandmother, and John stood a little back from the car ready to wave goodbye, when Jack went over to his grandfather. He pulled the driftwood *Petit Bateau* from his pocket and said simply, "You made me a boat, so I thought I should make you one too."

Epilogue

Jack didn't tell his parents much about the summer at the lake. He didn't tell them about rowing and finding sunfish nests. He didn't tell them about capsizing in the middle of the cove. He didn't tell them about sculling or being drawn into the creek at the south end of the cove. He didn't tell them about how one duckling probably had become dinner for a water snake or a heron and how he would always think that it had been his fault and how his stomach tightened when he thought about that. He didn't tell them very much about his summer on the cove because he didn't think they would understand.

Besides, he wasn't just a little kid anymore. He was stronger now. He knew how to row and sail and scull. His skin had turned a golden brown in the summer sun. He had become friends with the birds, fish, turtles, and all the other creatures of the cove. But, most importantly, he was now a skipper of his own boat.

On the drive to their new home, his parents told him about their move and the new house and the hard work they had done to get everything ready for Jack and his sister. As Jack listened to his parents, his mind wandered and he thought about next summer. He thought about seeing the baby turtles, the sunfish, and maybe a new hatch of mallard ducklings. He hoped *Petit Bateau* would remember him—she would. A boy and his small boat have a bond that can't be broken even by a long winter of snow and ice.

Life is about family and important gifts we give to those we love. It's about gifts that transform us and help us grow and gain a new, fresh perspective on life. It's a clever book given thoughtfully. It's garden seeds that will grow and bloom. It's art that stimulates fresh ideas and deep longing. It's, in this case, a small boat.

Glossary

Aft: toward the back end of a boat

Aft Seat: the seat toward the stern of a boat

Auger Post: a post that can be screwed into the sandy bottom of a lake

Belaying Pin: a pin or short rod used to secure a rope

Boom: a spar (pole) along the bottom edge of a sail

Bow: toward the front end of a boat

Bowline: a rope fastened to the front end of a boat

Bow Plate: a metal plate at the bow of a boat that protects the boat

Bow Seat: a seat toward the bow of a boat

Brightwork: wood on a boat that has been varnished

Clove Hitch: a knot used to secure a boat to a dock or post

Cove: a small, sheltered bay

Dacron: a manmade fiber used to make sails for boats

Dagger Board Trunk: a thin box by which a dagger board is supported in small boats

Dinghy: a small boat for rowing or sailing

Dock: a small pier coming out from the shore into a body of water to which boats can be moored

Feather the Oars: to bring an oar out of the water with the face of the blade parallel to the water

Gaff: a spar (pole) to which the top edge of a sail is secured

Grommet: an eyelet placed in a hole of a sail to protect a rope passed through it

Gunwale: the upper edge of the side of a boat

Keel-Rub Strake: in a wooden boat, a metal band running along the keel from one end of the boat to the other

Luffing: close to the wind to the point at which a sail just begins to flap

Mainsheet: a rope used to pull a sail in

Mast: a spar (pole) used to hold a sail up in a boat

Oar Blade: the flat, broad end of an oar that pulls through the water

Oar Leathers: leather wrapped around an oar to protect the wood from wear

Oar Lock: either a U-shaped or circular metal hoop secured in the gunwale used to hold an oar in place

Oar Stops: (usually) leather bands that keep a circular oar lock from sliding too far up an oar

Port: looking forward, the left side of a boat

Port Tack: sailing a boat with the sail on the starboard side of centerline

Rudder: a control surface below the water used to steer a boat

Sheer Plank: the top-most plank on each side of a boat

Spars: poles used for sail control and sailing

Glossary

Starboard: looking forward, the right side of a boat

Starboard Tack: sailing a boat with the sail on the port side of centerline

Stern Line: a rope fastened to the stern of a boat

Tiller: (usually) a thin lever (stick or pole) attached to a rudder used to steer a boat

Transom: the flat surface forming the stern of a vessel

Made in the USA
Middletown, DE
09 January 2018